"Here is our country. Cherish these natural wonders. Cherish these natural resources...
for your children, and your children's children."

– Theodore Roosevelt

Chickadeeland

*For my children and my children's children,
and for Donna, my love*

For All Our Children
Bill Siddall

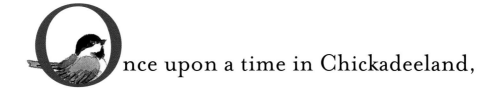nce upon a time in Chickadeeland,

Grandpa and Cora Lu
were up very late
and giggling very loud.
Others in the house had had enough.

Enough! Settle down! Time for bed!

"My, my,"
Grandpa winked.
"You heard what they said...

...hmmm, instead..."

Imagine!

We tiptoe outside
by a silver stream.
There's the moon!
Now follow the beam
to a magical place
beyond the river,
where fireflies sparkle
and tall trees shiver.

There!
Can you count
the holes
in all those trees?
Each hole
is a home
for chickadees.
They're sleeping now
(as you should be).

But here's what I wonder, strange as it seems,
what kind of dreams do chickadees dream?

Do they dream of the feast that Papa brings?
Of snuggling under Mama's wings?
Of singing like the nightingale sings?

Or do they dream

of SILLY things...

... like dancing a jig on ostrichy legs,

or laying ginormous ostrichy eggs?

Do they dream of hiding near bunny clouds,
far above admiring crowds?

Are they king and queen of the birdie parade, basking in flamingo shade,

munching fat tweetles and barbequed beetles,
and drinking from fountains
of wormalade?

Do they walk the plank, one by one, then swim with sharks just for fun?
Or do their dreams follow the sun...

in spring, dreams of color...

in summer, webbed feet...

in autumn, a costume...

in winter, the heat?!?!

And of all their dreams
great and small,
is the silliest,
daffodiliest dream of all

a loopy, hoopy, alley-oopy ride

on the epic brontosaurus slide?

Weeee... Ewwww... Ahhhhh... Eeeeee...

and from that slide, do they launch to the sky...

and sail with eagles and fly and fly on a soaring dream through

Chickadeeland, from coral reef to canyon grand...

from Rockies to Smokies to lighthouse shore,

through redwood and birch and sycamore...

over bears and geysers

and bears in dunes...

do they skim by moonlit wolves and loons...

through arches and caves...

to a big river bending ...

past ancient forest and glacier ending...

by native kiva and tower of stone...

Do they dream of flying where no one has flown?

Do they ZOOM by hoodoo and crater and dome,

then turn around and fly away home?

Home,
where chickadreams
come to rest,
in a little hole,
on a little nest,
not far from where
you lay your head—
with Big Bunny
on a small bed.

Now here's what I know, and your bunny knows too:

when those birds took flight, so did you.
Only the fearless heart of a child can follow a dream into the wild,
and your good heart will always be as brave as the bravest chicka…

… listen …

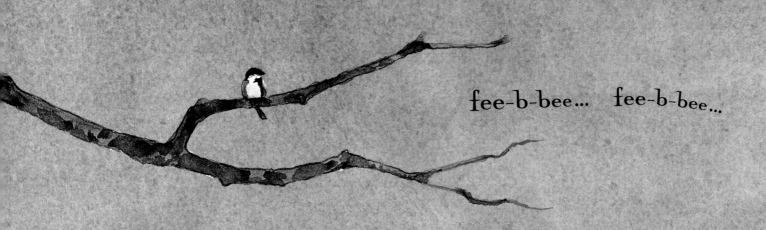

fee-b-bee...   fee-b-bee...

His still, small voice is our reminder:
We *must* be kinder.

Whatever his dreams,
wherever he flies,
we share the same trees.
We share the same skies.
From grizzliest bear to buzziest bee,
from wetland flower to desert tree,
to you and me and chickadees—
we share this land together.

So tonight, hug Big Bunny and I'll hug you.
Dream sweet dreams, and silly ones too.
Tomorrow, brave heart,
there's much to do, much to share...
magical places are everywhere!

Some Magical Places in
Chickadeeland

National Parks

1. Acadia
2. Arches
3. Badlands
4. Big Bend
5. Biscayne
6. Black Canyon
7. Bryce Canyon
8. Canyonlands
9. Capitol Reef
10. Carlsbad Caverns
11. Channel Islands
12. Congaree
13. Crater Lake
14. Cuyahoga Valley
15. Death Valley
16. Denali
17. Dry Tortugas
18. Everglades
19. Gates of the Arctic
20. Glacier
21. Glacier Bay
22. Grand Canyon
23. Grand Teton
24. Great Basin
25. Great Sand Dunes
26. Great Smoky Mountains
27. Guadalupe Mountains
28. Haleakala

29. Hawaiian Volcano
30. Hot Springs
31. Isle Royale
32. Joshua Tree
33. Katmai
34. Kenai Fjords
35. Kings Canyon
36. Kobuk Valley
37. Lake Clark
38. Lassen Volcanic
39. Mammoth Cave
40. Mesa Verde
41. Mount Rainier
42. American Samoa (not pictured)
43. North Cascades
44. Olympic

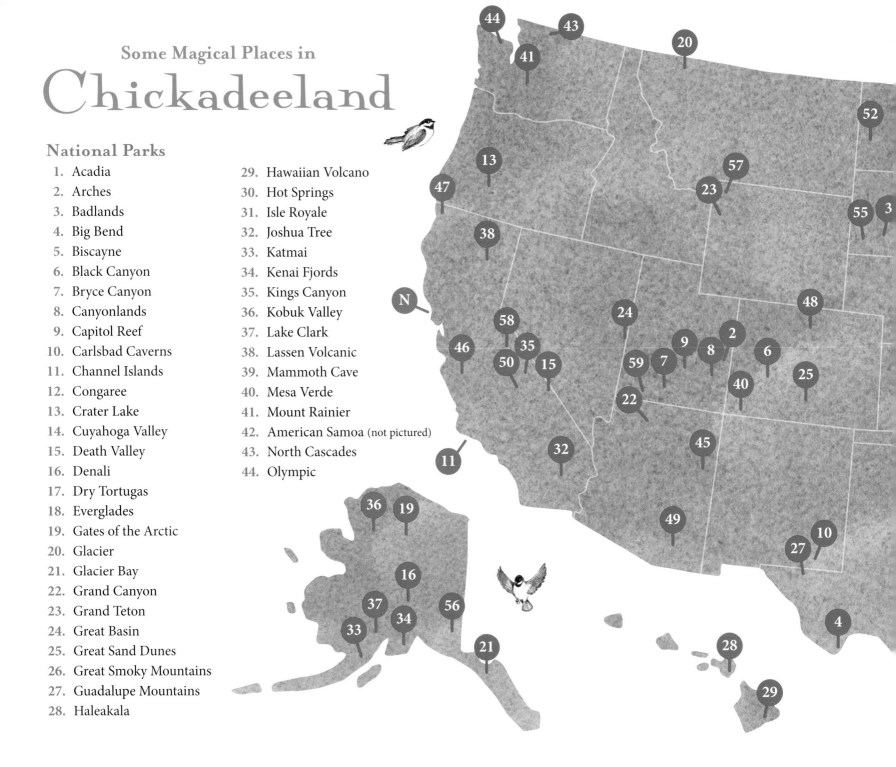

45. Petrified Forest
46. Pinnacles
47. Redwood
48. Rocky Mountain
49. Saguaro
50. Sequoia
51. Shenandoah
52. Theodore Roosevelt
53. Virgin Islands
54. Voyageurs
55. Wind Cave
56. Wrangell-St. Elias
57. Yellowstone
58. Yosemite
59. Zion

National Lakeshores

A. Apostle Islands
B. Indiana Dunes
C. Pictured Rocks
D. Sleeping Bear Dunes

National Seashores

E. Assateague Island
F. Canaveral
G. Cape Cod
H. Cape Hatteras
I. Cape Lookout
J. Cumberland Island
K. Fire Island
L. Gulf Islands
M. Padre Island
N. Point Reyes

Ten Questions about our Parks, Shores and Monuments

1. What national parks, shores, and monuments has your family visited?

2. Which ones are your favorites?

3. What is the only national monument shown in *Chickadeeland*?

4. When you visit a park, what do you like to see and hear?

5. What do you like to touch and smell?

6. Study the picture labeled "Glacier" on the next page. What is happening to the glacier and to the forest?

7. What little bird flies in every state in North America (and most parks)? *Big Hint: see book title!*

8. What national park, shore, or monument would you like to visit next?

9. In words or pictures, *Chickadeeland* celebrates at least twenty national parks and lakeshores. Can you name ten?

10. "Tomorrow, brave heart, there's much to do" is part of the last sentence of the story. Tomorrow, what can you do to help our parks or planet?

GLACIER

VOYAGEURS

GRAND CANYON

BISCAYNE

MOUNT RUSHMORE

Chickadeeland

by Bill O. Smith

illustrated by Charles R. Murphy

Text and Illustration Copyright © 2019 by Bill O. Smith

Book Design by Draw Big Design

Printed in the United States by Four Colour Print Group, Louisville, KY

Published by Sleepytime Press

E-mail: sleepytimepress@gmail.com

Web site: www.sleepytimepress.com

ISBN: 978-0-9895238-2-0
Library of Congress Control Number: 2018905352

"Never doubt that a small group of thoughtful, committed citizens can change the world;
indeed, it's the only thing that ever has."

– Margaret Mead